Sutton-at-Hone Library
Tel/Fax: 01322 863683 0719   suH

20. AUG 07
22. AUG 08.

01. SEP 08.

27. DEC 08.
21 MAR 2009

1 6 MAY 2009

- 6 JUN 2009

1 8 AUG 2009

1 2 SEP 2009

WITHDRAWN

2 9 DEC 2009

1 9 JUL 2019

-3 SEP 2010

1 5 APR 2011

0 6 MAY 2011   2 1 APR 2017

2 5 JUL 2016
1 8 JUN 2012
2 3 JUL 2012

3 0 DEC 2013

1 0 OCT 2014

Books should be returned or renewed by the
last date stamped above   1 2 JUN 2015

- 4 AUG 2017   0 7 AUG 2015

1 1 FEB 2019   2 6 OCT 2015   2 0 AUG 2018

2 2 AUG 2022

1 8 DEC 2015

Libraries & Archives

CHARTER MARK
CUSTOMER SERVICE EXCELLENCE

Kent County Council

D0278940

First published in 2006 by
Franklin Watts
338 Euston Road
London
NW1 3BH

Franklin Watts Australia
Hachette Children's Books
Level 17/207 Kent Street
Sydney
NSW 2000

Text © Hilary Robinson 2006
Illustration © Barbara Vagnozzi 2006

The rights of Hilary Robinson to be identified as the author
and Barbara Vagnozzi as the illustrator of this Work have
been asserted in accordance with the Copyright, Designs
and Patents Act, 1988.

All rights reserved. No part of this publication may be
reproduced, stored in a retrieval system, or transmitted
in any form or by any means, electronic, mechanical,
photocopy, recording or otherwise, without the prior
written permission of the copyright owner.

A CIP catalogue record for this book is available
from the British Library.

ISBN (10) 0 7496 6594 7 (hbk)
ISBN (13) 978-0-7496-6594-4 (hbk)
ISBN (10) 0 7496 6811 3 (pbk)
ISBN (13) 978-0-7496-6811-2 (pbk)

Series Editor: Jackie Hamley
Series Advisor: Dr Barrie Wade
Series Designer: Peter Scoulding

Printed in China

For Alex, Imogen and Thomas,
and Molly, who loves
rings and bling – H.R.

KENT
LIBRARIES & ARCHIVES
C153090153

The Royal
Jumble Sale

by Hilary Robinson

Illustrated by Barbara Vagnozzi

W
FRANKLIN WATTS
LONDON • SYDNEY

There was panic
in the palace

when the King
lost his ring.

The royal maids

were ordered

to search through
everything!

They emptied
all the cupboards.

They tipped out
all the drawers.

They searched
the royal laundry.

They combed
the palace floors.

The royal hanky
servant said:

"We must get on the trail.

13

"I fear it may have been sold ...

"... in the royal jumble sale!"

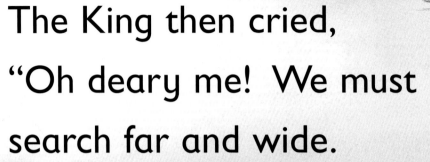

The King then cried,
"Oh deary me! We must
search far and wide.

17

"If a lady does return it,
she shall become my bride!"

So word soon spread throughout the land:

"Whoever finds the ring ...

"... will have a crown
of jewels and be
married to the King!"

A dairymaid then
found the ring
in the King's old
riding glove.

She'd bought them
for her father,

and now she was in love!

But at the royal wedding
as the King stood
in his gown,

panic set in once again ...

... the King had lost his crown!

Leapfrog has been specially designed to fit the requirements of the National Literacy Strategy. It offers real books for beginning readers by top authors and illustrators.

There are 55 Leapfrog stories to choose from:

The Bossy Cockerel
ISBN 0 7496 3828 1

Bill's Baggy Trousers
ISBN 0 7496 3829 X

Mr Spotty's Potty
ISBN 0 7496 3831 1

Little Joe's Big Race
ISBN 0 7496 3832 X

The Little Star
ISBN 0 7496 3833 8

The Cheeky Monkey
ISBN 0 7496 3830 3

Selfish Sophie
ISBN 0 7496 4385 4

Recycled!
ISBN 0 7496 4388 9

Felix on the Move
ISBN 0 7496 4387 0

Pippa and Poppa
ISBN 0 7496 4386 2

Jack's Party
ISBN 0 7496 4389 7

The Best Snowman
ISBN 0 7496 4390 0

Eight Enormous Elephants
ISBN 0 7496 4634 9

Mary and the Fairy
ISBN 0 7496 4633 0

The Crying Princess
ISBN 0 7496 4632 2

Jasper and Jess
ISBN 0 7496 4081 2

The Lazy Scarecrow
ISBN 0 7496 4082 0

The Naughty Puppy
ISBN 0 7496 4383 8

Freddie's Fears
ISBN 0 7496 4382 X

FAIRY TALES

Cinderella
ISBN 0 7496 4228 9

The Three Little Pigs
ISBN 0 7496 4227 0

Jack and the Beanstalk
ISBN 0 7496 4229 7

The Three Billy Goats Gruff
ISBN 0 7496 4226 2

Goldilocks and the Three Bears
ISBN 0 7496 4225 4

Little Red Riding Hood
ISBN 0 7496 4224 6

Rapunzel
ISBN 0 7496 6159 3

Snow White
ISBN 0 7496 6161 5

The Emperor's New Clothes
ISBN 0 7496 6163 1

The Pied Piper of Hamelin
ISBN 0 7496 6164 X

Hansel and Gretel
ISBN 0 7496 6162 3

The Sleeping Beauty
ISBN 0 7496 6160 7

Rumpelstiltskin
ISBN 0 7496 6165 8

The Ugly Duckling
ISBN 0 7496 6166 6

Puss in Boots
ISBN 0 7496 6167 4

The Frog Prince
ISBN 0 7496 6168 2

The Princess and the Pea
ISBN 0 7496 6169 0

Dick Whittington
ISBN 0 7496 6170 4

The Elves and the Shoemaker
ISBN 0 7496 6575 0*
ISBN 0 7496 6581 5

The Little Match Girl
ISBN 0 7496 6576 9*
ISBN 0 7496 6582 3

The Little Mermaid
ISBN 0 7496 6577 7*
ISBN 0 7496 6583 1

The Little Red Hen
ISBN 0 7496 6578 5*
ISBN 0 7496 6585 8

The Nightingale
ISBN 0 7496 6579 3*
ISBN 0 7496 6586 6

Thumbelina
ISBN 0 7496 6580 7*
ISBN 0 7496 6587 4

RHYME TIME

Squeaky Clean
ISBN 0 7496 6805 9

Craig's Crocodile
ISBN 0 7496 6806 7

Felicity Floss: Tooth Fairy
ISBN 0 7496 6807 5

Captain Cool
ISBN 0 7496 6808 3

Monster Cake
ISBN 0 7496 6809 1

The Super Trolley Ride
ISBN 0 7496 6810 5

The Royal Jumble Sale
ISBN 0 7496 6594 7*
ISBN 0 7496 6811 3

But, Mum!
ISBN 0 7496 6595 5*
ISBN 0 7496 6812 1

Dan's Gran's Goat
ISBN 0 7496 6596 3*
ISBN 0 7496 6814 8

Lighthouse Mouse
ISBN 0 7496 6597 1*
ISBN 0 7496 6815 6

Big Bad Bart
ISBN 0 7496 6599 8*
ISBN 0 7496 6816 4

Ron's Race
ISBN 0 7496 6600 5*
ISBN 0 7496 6817 2

* hardback